Mr. Flying Cicada

Keep Trying... Keep Flying!

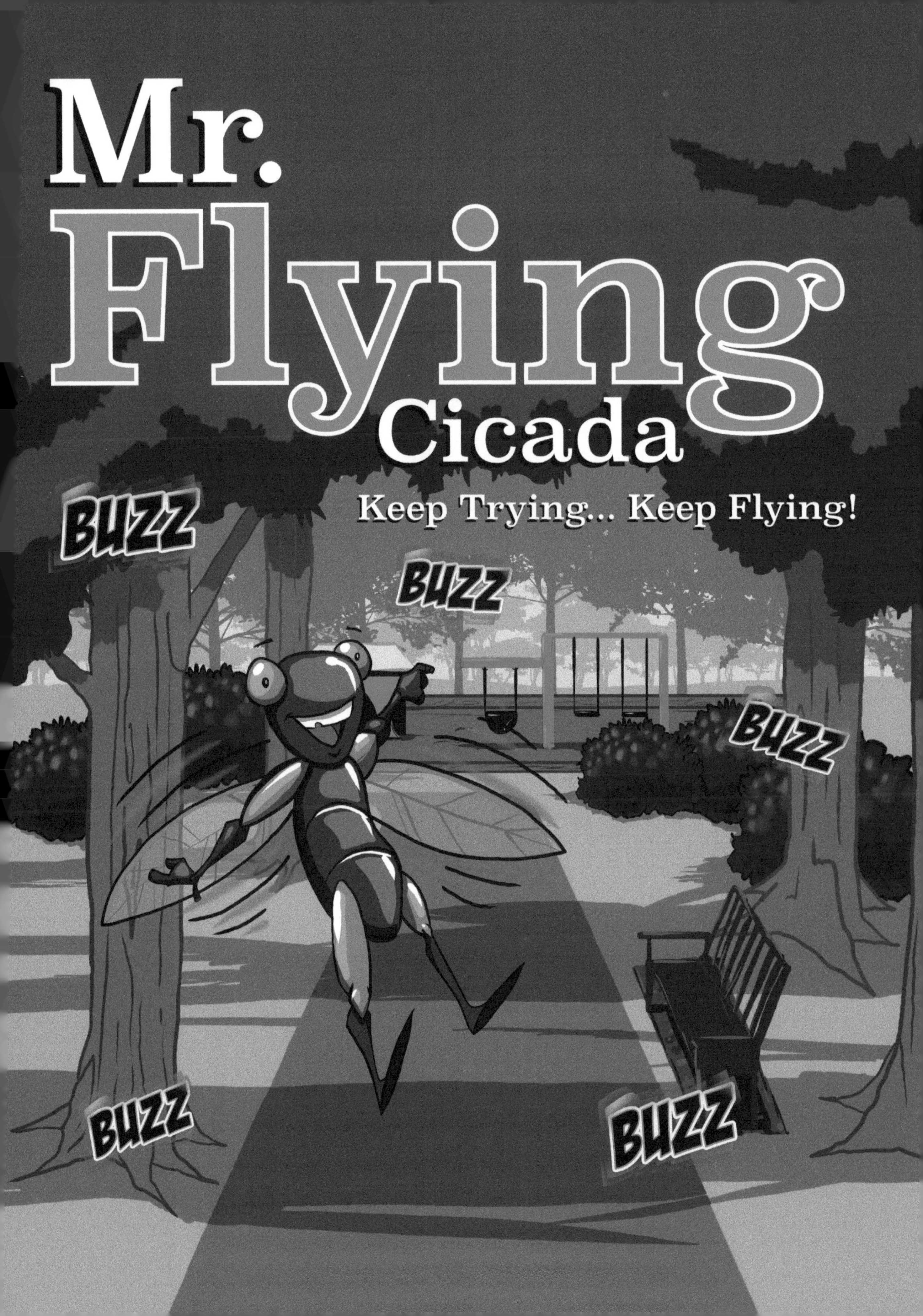

Mr. Flying Cicada

www.lfbookpublishing.com

Summary: *Mr. Flying Cicada* is primarily a children's book, but its message is applicable in all aspects of life. It details the journey of a cicada who struggles to fly. Eventually, he finds the courage to fly through encouragement from his new friend, Robin. The spirit of Mr. Flying Cicada is awakened in us ..when we keep trying ...we keep flying. Don't ever, ever give up..

ISBN: 978-1-7348113-9-1

In the Rose Garden, I sit. It is beautiful here and there is a noise, a buzz, close by and far away. Can you hear the sound of the buzz?

In the Rose Garden where there is dirt, you can see the holes from where they came from. There are lots of shells that look like the size of the cicadas.

Cicadas make this buzz. There are many cicadas around me…but the one that just landed on my shoulder is special! I said to the cicada… "My name is Robin."

I looked over my shoulder. He smiled and said to me…
"I am trying to fly!"

I picked him up gently and tossed him in the air. He flew away saying.. "Look at me! I am flying!"

He flew to the tree and looked at me saying.. "Thanks for the help!" I wondered how high he could fly?

He landed on the tree and yelled back at me… "I am Mr. Flying Cicada. It's a short life! All of my friends are laying around … on the ground.. and on the path."

Mr. Flying Cicada shouted…. "Help me to fly! Do you think I can fly higher?" I said .. "Of course!" Mr. Flying Cicada said… "Thanks Robin! I really appreciate you!"

Mr. Flying Cicada said.. "Your kind words help me! If I fly, I am busy and I think I can live longer!" Robin said.. "Mr. Flying Cicada, you will be a good example for all your friends laying around!"

There is another one! It just flew and fell right out of the sky. I don't know why? One might think with big wings he could keep flying!

There is a little girl swinging close by. She yells…
"Cicada! Cicada! Cicada!"

Joining the cicadas buzzing sounds of praise, the birds sing in the trees. Mr. Sparrow says.. "Mr. Cicada..you can do it! Fly like me!"

OK.. "Call me ..Mr Flying Cicada…please!"

Mr. Flying Cicada just flew back to me..as another fell..right out of the sky..zig zagging..and landing upside down..SPLAT!

"Will you be my friend Mr. Flying Cicada? That is your name from now on because you keep trying! Fly high and fly low! You can land on my shoulder anytime!"

Ms. Bumblebee was moving about a flower petal. She yelled at Mr. Flying Cicada.. "If you don't eat, you won't have energy to fly like me! Keep trying! Keep flying!"

Mr. Flying Cicada thanked Ms. Bumblebee for her kind words. He said.. "I really appreciate you! I don't know how you do it? Your wings are smaller than mine."

"Don't worry!" exclaimed Mr. Flying Cicada; "I won't sit on your shoulder too long. I have to go cheer on my friends laying on the ground!"

A very small ladybug flew up and landed on a rose. She said..
"Keep trying! Keep flying! I am Lady LadyBug!"

Mr. Squirrel was bothering the bird house next to the tree, but he took time to say.. "Keep trying..Keep flying!"

I think Mr. Flying Cicada and his family of cicada friends like warm weather. The warmer it gets, the louder the buzz becomes.

I thought I heard the statue of Saint Francis of Assisi whisper.. "Dearest Mr. Flying Cicada..I beg of thee..Don't stop trying! Keep flying! God gave you a great pair of wings! Use them my good friend!"

You can still hear the buzz up close and far away. One day the buzz will stop and not begin again for a long time.

Be like Mr. Flying Cicada…Keep Trying! Keep Flying!

Author

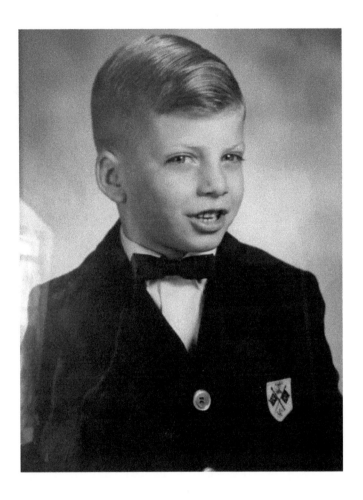

Of all my jobs .. from US Marines, GNC Franchise Owner (California, Virginia, Washington DC) and Real Estate, nothing compares to my time spent during 2010 to 2012 as a substitute teacher. Having taught in over half of the schools in the Fairfax County Public School System, I witnessed first hand, the loving care of our teachers who are always in the trenches trying...I also witnessed, as well, the beauty reflected in God's creation through His children... our students. With humility comes great service. Tim has been married to Lisa for 32 years and has four children: Matthew, Rachel, Rebecca and Jacob.

Dedication

This book is dedicated to Robin Miller. He was a friend of mine since high school. He fell on hard times later in life and lived in the woods his last 12 years as the poorest of the poor. He never gave up and always kept trying amidst his great suffering. In May, 2021, He was hit and killed by a car in the evening while walking to the store to get gas for his generator.

CPSIA information can be obtained
at www.ICGtesting.com
Printed in the USA
LVHW020736231021
701271LV00002B/19